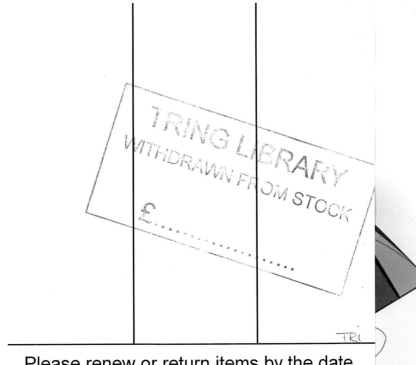

Please renew or return items by the date shown on your receipt

www.hertfordshire.gov.uk/libraries

Renewals and enquiries: 0300 123 4049

Textphone for hearing or 0300 123 4041
speech impaired users:

Hertfordshire

SHWE A AGGARWAL
SOMNATH CHATTERJEE

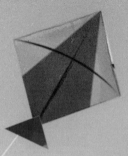

Dev and Ollie

Kite Crazy!

First published by Curious Minds Press Ltd in 2015
ISBN-13: 978-0-993-2328-0-0
ISBN-10: 0993232809

Text and Illustration copyright Curious Minds Press Ltd 2015
Moral rights asserted.

Curious Minds Press

www.devandollie.com

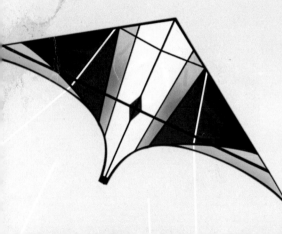

To everyone
who's crazy about something!

INTRODUCING...

Dev

Cheeky, clumsy
and very curious.
A HUGE football fan.

Ollie

Dev's magical cuddly
toy. Always eager to
take off on adventures.

Grandpa

Claims to be an expert
at almost everything!

The Old Man

Spent his whole life
making kites!

Rahul

Is simply kite crazy!

Rahul's Father

Quite a serious fellow
but a nice guy really.

Dev zoomed around his room with his kite. It was his favourite birthday present. There was only one problem...

rrrrr...

...he didn't know how to fly it! Just then, Grandpa walked in.

"That's not how you fly a kite dear," chuckled Grandpa. "I was an expert. I'll teach you tomorrow."

"Now Grandpa," begged Dev.

"Tomorrow," said Grandpa tucking Dev into bed.

Dev was almost asleep when Ollie, his magical bedtime owl, came alive.

"Come with me on a journey and we'll surprise Grandpa tomorrow morning," whispered Ollie.

Curious, Dev hopped on board
with droopy eyes and off they went.

Minutes later...

...the sky was **full** of kites!! Avoiding them all...

...they **crash-landed** on the roof terrace
of a family home, onto a pile of kites.

They had arrived at Gujarat's kite festival.

As Dev dusted himself off,
he heard a little boy cry,
"You broke my kite!"

"Rahul, we'll get you another
one," said the boy's father.

"Uh-oh!" said Dev.
"I'll bring you my kite."

But it wasn't just one kite.
They had broken **all** the
kites!

Dev promised Rahul he'd
replace them and flew out
again with Ollie.

In a flash, they arrived in Patang Bazaar. They saw many shops with hundreds of colourful kites. The shops looked very busy, **all except one...**

...an old man's shop. No one was buying any kites from him!

"Gosh, your shop could do with tidying up," said Dev.

"If I help, could you help me?"

"Of course!" replied the old man.
"All I have is kites. Would that help?"

"Perfect!" smiled Dev.

He whizzed around, neatly arranging
all the kites and dusting the cobwebs.

"Working hard Dev!" said Ollie.
"If only you tidied up your room
like this."

"No way!" said Dev.
"This is much more fun."

Almost done, Dev placed a ladder
to reach the mess on the top shelf when suddenly...

..."Mouse!"
he screamed.

The ladder tipped, Dev fell and several trophies came tumbling down on his head!

Those trophies belonged to the old man. He turned out to be a **champion** kite flyer! Dev had an idea. He placed the trophies at the entrance of the shop and invited everyone on the street to come in.

Soon there was a big queue outside. The old man was over the moon!

Dev returned to Rahul with a few special kites
the old man had given him.

"Wow, thanks!" said Rahul.

Rahul started flying his kite straight away while Dev watched carefully.

"Kai po che!" yelled Rahul.

"Kai po what?" asked Dev.

"It means 'I've cut your kite string'," laughed Rahul.

"That's naughty!" said Dev.

"Let me explain," said Rahul's father.

"In kite matches, you entangle your kite string with someone else's kite. Then you tug on your string until eventually one kite string is cut and that kite drifts away."

"Ah, it's like kite tug of war. Can I 'kai po che' a kite?" asked Dev.

"Of course," said Rahul. Dev eagerly grabbed the string.
This was the moment he'd been waiting for.

Then, suddenly...SPLAT!!! A pigeon dropping landed on his hand.

"Maybe you'll have better luck against Grandpa," chuckled Ollie.

"He'll be up soon."

"I'd better get going," said Dev.

"**Wait!**" said Rahul's father. "This is for you."

Dev thanked him. Then he took off with Ollie to return home.

As they were leaving Gujarat, they saw thousands
of candle-lit kites filling the night sky.

'It's like the stars have come down!" said Dev
reaching out to grab one.

"Be careful! Below us is the Salt Desert of Kutch!" said Ollie.

"Salt desert?" asked Dev.

"Yes, the largest in the world," said Ollie swooping down.
Dev scraped the surface and licked the salt off his finger.

"Yuck, definitely salt!!" he spluttered.

Stretching for
miles, there
were glowing
kites
above...

...and a glittering surface below. Dev fell asleep enjoying the view.

In the morning, Dev **burst** into Grandpa's room.
"Wake up Grandpa, let's have a kite match!" said Dev.

"But we only have one kite," said Grandpa.
"I was given another one," said Dev.
Grandpa quickly joined Dev in the garden.

Surprised, Grandpa watched Dev prepare the kites.

"Have you been up practising all night?" he asked.

"Concentrate Grandpa or you'll lose," smiled Dev.
Their kite strings were entangled tightly.
Dev pulled hard on his string.

"Yes! I did it!" yelled Dev.

Grandpa's kite was cut and drifted away.

Dev heard Ollie whisper something
and suddenly Dev shouted,
"Kai po che!"

"Well done! Now, shall we go and tidy up **your** room?"
teased Ollie.

Facts For Curious Minds

◆ Gujarat's Kite Festival, Uttarayan, is also an international festival which attracts kite lovers from all over the world. Every year on the 14th of January, millions of kite flyers in India are seen on roof tops and open fields, flying kites day and night, to celebrate the end of winter and the beginning of harvest season.

◆ During this festival, Patang Bazaar is open 24 hours!

◆ In the day, the sky in Gujarat is full of colourful kites. At night, people release glowing candle lit kites called Tukkals. Tukkals are like mini hot air balloons.

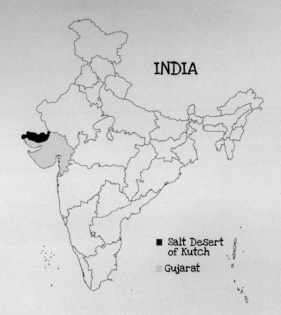

INDIA

■ Salt Desert of Kutch
▪ Gujarat

◆ Kite trains can be created with hundreds of kites on a single string! A smaller version is on the front cover. Can you count how many there are? Mind Ollie's belly!

◆ Kites were first developed in ancient China more than 2000 years ago. In fact, it is now thought that the first kites flown over 3000 years ago, were made from leaves.

◆ The aeroplane is a development of the kite.

◆ There are 78 rules in kite fighting in Thailand.

◆ More adults in the world fly kites than children.

◆ Each year on the second Sunday of October kite flyers in nearly every country unite and fly a kite to celebrate "ONE SKY ONE WORLD".

◆ The Salt Desert in Kutch is underwater during the monsoon season. For the rest of the year, it's a great stretch of salt, really!!

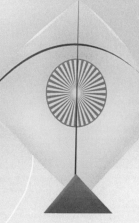

Have you thought about what you would like
for your next birthday present?

A kite maybe ?

How many times can you spot Ollie?

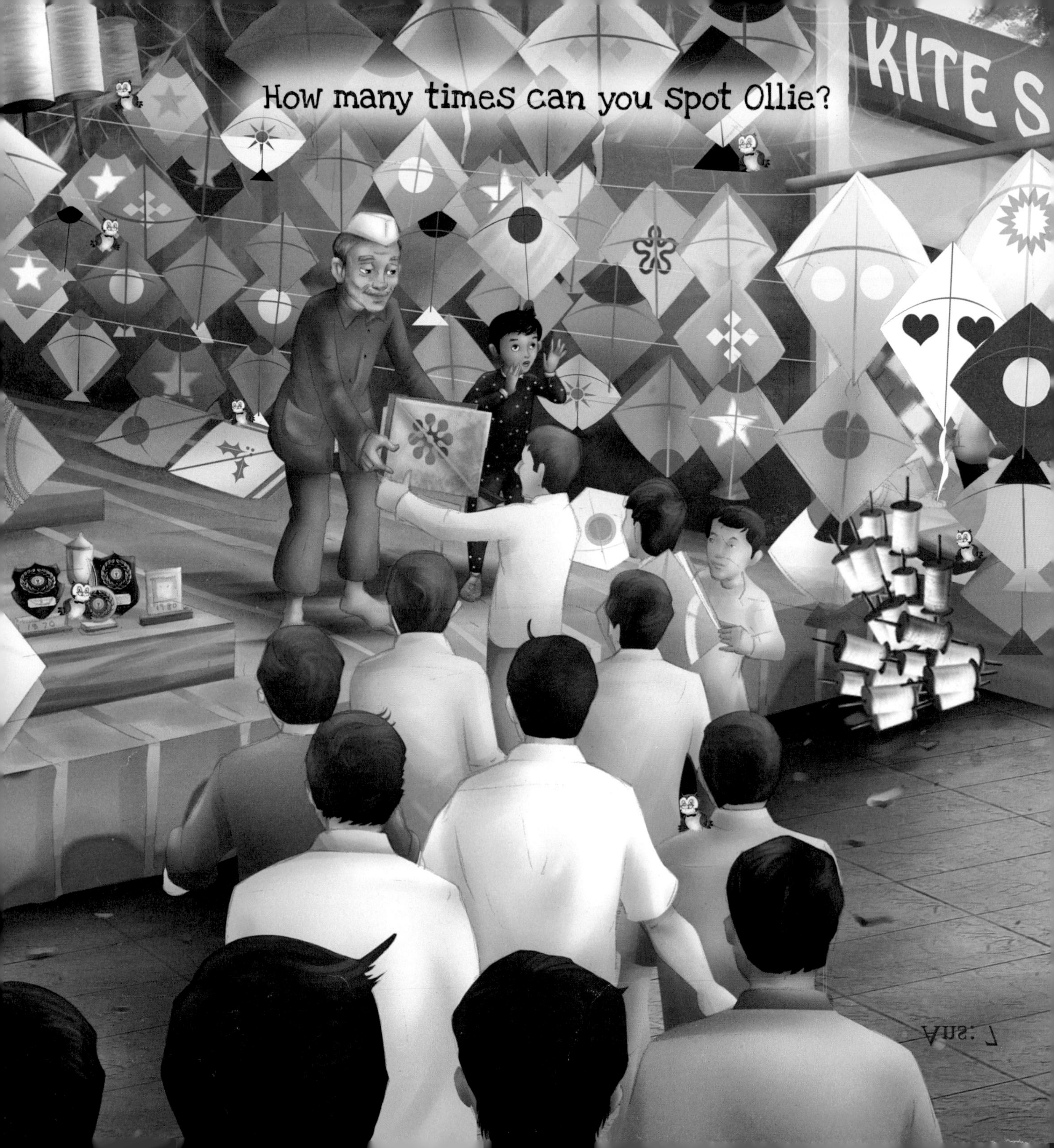

Ans: 7